SheyA's Quest

DEDICATION

This edition is dedicated to my parents Marthe L. Ulysse and Jean C. Ulysse. May your Souls and hearts be elevated exponentially each time this book is touched.

CHAPTERS

Acknowledgments

1 Heartland
2 The Out'hers
3 Lost
4 Amber-The River Goddess
5 The Cave Guardian
6 Re-awakening
7 Heart Resurrection
8 Sun of God
9 Finding Wisdom and Going Home

ACKNOWLEDGMENTS

I give thanks to my Source of continuous guidance and all who supported me on this project.

1 HEARTLAND

Imagine living in a part of an inner world that was visible only temporarily and only to some. Although many had heard of it, few have seen it. Before I go on, let me say first and foremost, this land itself is not central to our story, because this story could happen anywhere. This land heartland was mystical to those who lived outside its boundaries but simple to those who live within.

In heartland was a young light being called SheyA. And for our purpose, SheyA's light lived, died and lived again and that was all that she needed to know.

SheyA never knew how she came to be and frankly, she never wondered about it. There were many other light beings just like her in HeartLand, and they lived harmoniously. As far as she could tell, these were beings of light as long as anyone could remember.

SheyA and the other light beings had this ritual where they would speak to their hearts every moment of the day and through the eve. "Good morning heart. How are you today heart? Where should I go? What should I do?" SheyA and every light in HeartLand never lived a moment without connecting with their hearts. What's even more interesting, is that they also waited patiently to hear their heart's response. And the heart would always respond with sage advice that would always guide them home.

As a result of this constant communication with the heart, all inhabitants had everything they needed and sometimes even before they thought of it. It was magical. SheyA would go wherever she wanted to and always seemed to get back home just in time. She never rushed and never feared. She never worried and never thought. She simply was SheyA.

In HeartLand there was no fear, no war, and no hate. The way SheyA's world existed was different from this parallel world. In HeartLand, there was only one light shared by many, and so eventually it was known that all would return to it. The shadow was also one source, not many, and it was not seen separated from, but complimentary to the light. The shadow cradled the light as it does in the sky. Neither was good nor bad. In HeartLand there was no duality, just co-existence between light and dark, as it is in space. The universe, the galaxy casts no shadow but exists in complete darkness. No one knows how this works, but without the dark matter in space for the light to rest, a light would cease to exist in space or HeartLand.

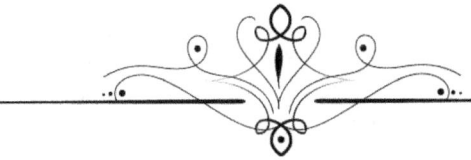

2 THE OUT'HERS

SheyA was young compared to others in her village. She was maybe 600 years old. Like most teenagers her age, she didn't know that there were other beings in a nearby village called Out'hers. The Out'hers lived in a parallel world, and although they had their rituals, they did not often do this ritual of the heart which was so common in HeartLand. And when they did, it was for a very short time--maybe a few seconds at the most. These Out'hers would sometimes travel through SheyA's community very quickly, almost at the speed of light. They would pass so quickly that SheyA's people would sometimes say it was because Out'hers occasionally spoke and listened to their hearts. The reason SheyA's people could not see the Out'hers except at light speed is that the Heartland dwellers were connected so strongly to their hearts. The disconnected Shado of the parallel world (another name HearLanders gave to the Out'hers), could not remain present long enough to be visible to them. Only when one or the other stopped or changed its ritual for a very long time, could the invisible become visible? Only when something went drastically different for a very long time, could a HeartLander cross over to the parallel world.

As years passed, SheyA became more aware of the Out'hers world around her. No one knows how this started. SheyA began to notice that sometimes other lights beings passed by slower than others. Mesmerized by the light show, SheyA would stop talking to her heart to try and catch another "light show," as she sometimes called it. After some time had passed, things began to shift and seem different; these light shows appeared to move slower and slower. They also have a shaded body with all kinds of "stuff" attached to it. Some had a lot. One even had stuff that towered several feet high. The more stuff, the harder it was to see a light show. But they all had a light of some kind; some were just dimmer or different colors than the others. The Out'hers always seemed to move in a pattern which helped to create beautiful colors. SheyA noticed when they moved faster; certain patterns would appear. Some patterns were more hypnotic and almost seemed to put SheyA in a trance. She would stop talking to her heart for hours and not notice anything but the lights. But, thank goodness, the Shado never stayed, and SheyA would eventually speak to her heart and returned home.

However, with each passing day, SheyA followed the other lights further and further away. Those in her community noticed her light was dimming and that she stopped talking to her heart, but the beings in her community did not interfere. It was not their custom for they knew SheyA, like all others before her, must find her path and would eventually return home. They seemed to know something SheyA did not, and they remembered the time when she would discover this truth was soon to come.

This distancing continued for years, and SheyA began to seek these Out'hers religiously, thus neglecting herself and most importantly her heart. She no longer felt her heartbeat or heard its song. Her light dimmed more and more, and the Out'hers appeared clearer and clearer to her. The Shado were now mostly bodies with shaded lights. But there was something else. They began to manifest faces, or rather masks that looked like faces. These masks or faces showed a mixture of different emotions at once. Most were wearing happy smiles with sad eyes or laughing smiles with angry or confused eyes. These Out'hers were confusing to SheyA, but she could not stop herself.

Until one day. One day out of curiosity, SheyA left her community and followed these shaded figures. No one knows for how long she followed them, but it must have been a very long time. For SheyA appeared to be able to see more than a light show. But as time passed, something had also changed inside of SheyA. She began to notice the shaded figures changing forms and becoming denser. The more she looked for these Out'hers, the less she remembered about herself. She did not notice when she stopped talking to her heart. But at some point, she stopped and forgot she had a heart. She also forgot she had a light inside of her. Eventually, she stopped returning home and stayed with the Shado.

The more she looked at these beings, the more real they appeared to her. She began to feel as if she forgot something critical, but couldn't say what it was. Day in and day out, these Out'hers would pass by and they began to wander closer to SheyA. SheyA now noticed they wore clothes, lots, and lots of colorful clothes. They also appeared to have no sense of purpose and no longer moved in a pattern but in a confused, lost misdirected way. But at a closer look that too was a pattern, just not one anyone may want to follow.

Then one day, SheyA noticed that some of the younger Out'hers also began to see her too. Up until then, she had not been visible to them. One of the youngest ones looked at her suspiciously for a long time while trying to get the attention of an adult Out'hers.

Some days later, a child with a funny mask face pointed straight at SheyA and began to laugh hysterically. Immediately, SheyA felt her body fill with a sharp pain in her chest--a feeling she had never felt before.

The Shado child continued to laugh while pointing at SheyA. SheyA felt this hurt, but the child would not stop laughing. The more she laughed, the more SheyA noticed that she, too, was becoming denser. She began to resemble these Shado people. She noticed she too wore clothes, but her clothes felt dirty against her skin. Skin, she had never noticed that before. Her feet ached from all her walking. How long had she walked? Feet? She had never noticed before. SheyA looked down and saw she also had hands. And they looked old and cracked. Hands, she had never needed those before. The laughter stopped.

SheyA looked around her, and for the first time she saw a place around her, she did not recognize. She began to feel this odd sensation of being alone, vulnerable and scared. Feelings she had never experienced before. She also felt she was different from the Out'hers, who were all the same. This realization caused her pain in the center of her body--pain she had never felt before then.

She wanted to make this pain go away. For a brief moment, she remembered her friend, her confidante, her guide, her heart and she screamed out loud, "Heart, what is wrong with me?"

Silence. Then her heart whispered. "I don't understand this SheyA, but I will help you find out."

Before SheyA could say another word, a little boy mask in a man's body said to her, "You. You are all wrong. Yes, you. You do not have a mask. What is the matter with you? You are not wearing clothes that cover that thing inside of you. You. You are alone. And yes, you. You are just a scared, pathetic old hag. You do not belong here. You are wrong."

The voice vanished with the boy mask vanishing with it. And SheyA fell again. Her heart sank deeper into her body. She noticed her light still present, so she covered it up with her old clothes, so no one else would notice her. And SheyA slept.

3 LOST

Difficult to say how long, but some in HeartLand say SheyA must have slept for a minute or two, but Shado folks say it was a long time, maybe years. Thump! SheyA felt a loud thump in her chest and woke up. She looked around and saw she was in this strange place, but reminded herself that she must try getting back home.

As soon as that last word formed in her mind, she noticed some glittery rocks on the ground. She thought the Out'hers must have left these. At a closer look, they were not rocks at all, but beautiful jewels of all different sizes and colors. An anxious feeling came to her. I must find the Out'hers and ask them how I can have these jewels and become more like them. My light inside is not useful to me anymore. I must find the Out'hers first.

So, SheyA followed this trail, never stopping once to look up. The Shado say hours turned into days and days turned into weeks and weeks into months. But we know it may not have been so.

When SheyA finally looked up, she did not know where she was. She was so far into the Shado world. She knew she could not just turn around to get back home.

Then she saw another light not too far away. It was much bigger than the jewels she had been captivated by before. For a moment she thought it must be one of her HeartLand family. It must be one of her people, so she ran toward it. But as she got closer, she realized it was on the ground, and it was not moving. And it got smaller and smaller.

It was another golden gift left by the Out'hers - a mirror. SheyA had never seen a mirror before. In HeartLand, whenever she desired to see herself, she would look into her heart. Yes, her heart. SheyA remembered her heart for a moment, her heart always helped her find the answer. But she quickly dismissed the feeling, picked up the mirror and looked into it. And for the first time, she saw herself the way the Out'hers saw her. She looked old, dirty and weak. She wept. She wept, and she fell asleep again. This time, Shados still say she slept even longer than the last. But we in Heartland know that's not the case.

Thump! Thump! SheyA awakened by that thump sound from her heart. Again, she remembered she had her heart still with her, and even though she could not see it anymore, it was still beating inside her. So she asked her heart to help her find her way home. But first, she wanted to feel and have all these things she saw in the Out'hers. She could not bear to return home looking the way she was. Her time lost had turned her into this monster, and she could not go back to HeartLand this way.

Her heart was quiet. And said nothing.

Her heart did not understand SheyA's concerns since it knew her appearance had nothing do with anything.

SheyA screamed as loud as she could. "Please help me! I'm tired of being sad, alone, and scared! Help me find these people and get these things! I want to find the Out'hers and bring some of these jewels back home! My light has dimmed, and I can't go back this way!"

She then heard a soft, almost inaudible voice from above, around and below say, "Tell your heart your desires, and listen to your heart for the way home."

"What? What did you say," SheyA asked?

"Speak to your heart and your heart will guide you home."

"But I don't want to go back yet. Not like this. Please help me find beauty, youth, and treasures to take home. Help me locate these Out'hers and give me the courage to travel through the Shado's land." Everything was still silent. The voice had spoken and had nothing more to say. It was up to SheyA to act, and she knew it.

SheyA put her head down toward her heart and asked her

heart in a gentle voice. "Please help me find these things and then return me home. I am sick and tired of feeling like this. Help me find all these things and please help me find wisdom along the way too, so I never make this mistake and get this lost ever again."

Her heart responded softly, "SheyA, my beloved, to find what you are looking for, you will need to go on a quest. Because of the path you've taken so far, this is now your only way to these things you seek."

"What about," asked SheyA?

The heart said, "You will also find Wisdom along the way, and then I will guide you home."

So SheyA began to follow her heart again, reluctantly.

"Walk RIGHT and walk until you can walk no more," said her heart. So SheyA walked and walked and walked.

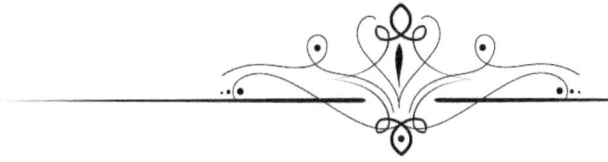

4 AMBER – THE RIVER GODDESS

SheyA grew so thirsty and tired that she thought she was going to die. But she kept going and eventually found the river with colors of Amber. Without asking her heart what to do, she jumped in head first. The water was so golden on top and felt so good that she lay on top and began to float and enjoy the healing coatings of amber shades.

SheyA did not realize that as she lay there with her eyes closed, she sank deeper and deeper. She drifted toward the bottom. As she sank deeper into the water, it became murky and dark. Suddenly, SheyA heard and felt a loud sound and turned toward it. That was when AMBER appeared--the River Goddess in a full body halo of amber light, adorned in a beautiful cloth of white and pink hues, with riches as far as one could see underneath her, in her hair, in her clothes, and her hands. She was beautiful, and SheyA was mesmerized.

But then SheyA's ears felt like they had exploded as AMBER

spoke with a voice that was unexpected. Her voice was shatteringly loud and with each word she emphasized, her eyes bulged out of their sockets.

"Seeker, I have the answers you desire." "Seeker, you desire wealth and beauty, am I right?"

SheyA was too scared to speak and trembled as she tried to swim back up. But she was unable to move.

"Seeker, answer me. You seek wealth and beauty, am I RIGHT?"

"Yes," SheyA mumbled.

"Then you must stay HERE; keep me company for as long as I DESIRE. I will tell you my STORIES, and in return, I will quench your THIRST and give you RICHES beyond your heart's desires."

Terrified, SheyA thought this was a good time to ask her heart what to do.

So SheyA looked down at her heart and asked softly, "What should I do?"

Her heart quickly responded, "You must stay with her SheyA, not for the riches, but because she wishes to be heard, and I cannot reject her."

"I cannot" said SheyA. "She is going to kill me with her voice and terror."

Her heart answered, "No she will not. But only if you promise to listen to her stories without judgment and learn from her errors."

"But what about my ears?" asked SheyA.

"You will no longer need them," answered her heart.

So SheyA agreed to stay and descended further into the abyss.

There, the Shados say, she remained for three years, three months, three days. But we know that is only partly right.

As the River Goddess shared her final story with SheyA, she noticed that her voice had grown so much softer and they had somehow floated up toward the darkest part of the water. They were close to shore, and SheyA could see the river bank.

"Go now--I have no more stories to tell you." said the River Goddess, who now appeared beautiful and gentle and kind. SheyA felt her beauty inside her heart.

To reward her for staying with her, AMBER gave SheyA three rings from her treasure chest and asked her to put them on her right fingers. With those rings, SheyA would be able to have riches beyond her heart's desire.

SheyA began to leave. AMBER stopped her and said, "SheyA, because you were so patient and kind to your AMBER, the

River Goddess, I will give you three more gifts."

You will now be able to not only hear when others speak with their mouths, but you will also now listen to what is hidden in others' hearts.

Out'hers' voices will never again hurt you. And you will never again fall into despair, no matter how painful your experience may appear."

SheyA climbed completely out of the river and rested. She looked down at her heart and checked to see if it was still there. She asked her heart for guidance. "Where do I go next?" Her heart said, go LEFT and walk as far as you can walk until you can't walk anymore.

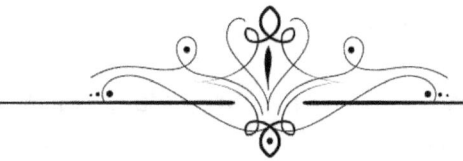

5 THE CAVE GUARDIAN

SheyA walked and walked and became so tired, hungry and lonely for other people and companionship; she thought she was going to die.

She sat down on a rock and rested. It was then; she noticed the Cave Guardian protecting his cave and the captives he called his cave family and his clan. Before she could speak, she heard him say without moving his lips, "Because you looked so tired, hungry and lost. Share my cave and my community. YOU and only YOU are welcome here."

"I have answers to your questions and food to feed your hungry belly," enticed the Cave Guardian.

He also added that he would allow members of his family and his clan to keep SheyA company each day, so she would never be alone again. SheyA did not understand how she could hear him without his mouth moving.

The Cave Guardian added, "But--before you can enter my

cave, I must initiate you into my clan."

SheyA looked into the cave and could make out a vast group of people. They were all unclothed and appeared emaciated. Their faces had a shape but no features she could make out. No eyes to see, no ears to hear, no nose to smell, and no mouth to speak. These Cave people had no faces. "Who are they?" SheyA asked. "You know them; they are the Out'hers. You've been looking for them, yes?"

SheyA wondered how he knew this. As if he could read her heart, he responded, "In this land SheyA, I know you better than you know yourself. Join us! The cave is where you belong."

The emptiness of her hungry belly coupled with finding the Out'hers-- in spite of their appearance here--tempted SheyA to stay, eat and rest. She needed company and remembered they were the only ones who might know how she could acquire all of those beautiful things she had seen.

So SheyA walked over to the cave. As she approached the entrance, the Cave Guardian stopped her and chuckled, "Well then, your initiation begins."

Oh yes, the initiation, SheyA recalled awkwardly. "What must I do?"

Without saying a word, he walked her over to a pile of "stuff" near the cave. Everything you could imagine was in this pile of stuff, including the gems she now remembered seeing on her journey. SheyA began to realize that this collection of things seemed to go on endlessly. There was no seeing around it or above it. So she stepped back and looked up. She noticed that what she was looking at was the bottom of a monstrously large pyramid that seemed to rise endlessly toward a point beyond the clouds. So this is where the stuff comes from? She thought. These are initiation sacrifices made by those who enter the cave.

The Cave Guardian added, "To be fed, everyone must give up their valuables as a sacrifice. You must also give up all your senses-- your hearing, your sight, your smell and your taste.

"WHAT?" questioned SheyA in a state of fear and confusion.

Without an excuse for this strangely demanding request, the Cave Guardian added, "in return, my cave will feed your stomach the best foods in this world. You will never need anything else."

Before she could think, he added, "You do not need a mouth to eat here. The cave will feed your stomach directly. You will be able to eat all you desire. But, as long as you feel full and satisfied, you would not be able to leave the cave. The only way the cave will allow you to move on is if you stopped feeding and only when you no longer sought to be part of the Out'hers. Then we would return your stuff to you."

SheyA was horrified. Give up everything before going in. And to get out, she must give up the Out'hers she had been seeking for so long! "Yes. Everything going in and everything coming out," replied the Cave Guardian.

SheyA thought a little longer and, remembering her jewels she said, "You did say I can have my stuff back, right?"

"Yes," replied the Cave Guardian. "SheyA, SheyA! You worry too much. You will never be hungry and lonely again. The cave will feed you, shelter you, and keep you in good company. You belong here."

SheyA thought for a moment. It all seemed to make sense. And besides, SheyA was hungry, tired and felt so alone. She would feed herself, enjoy some company, and then when she was satisfied; she would stop eating for a while and leave. She would take her jewels and go home.

Valuables! She thought. Besides her jewels, she had no other valuables. She started this quest with only the clothes on her back and later, the rings the River Goddess gave her.

She checked within for guidance and her heart told her to give away all she had-- her clothes, rings, and her senses. It also reminded her that she had special hearing gifted by the River Goddess so she can hear a lot more. But before she could thank her heart, it added, "I cannot survive in this cave SheyA. No one in the cave is real. With your senses gone, you will not be able to feel much, if anything. I will surely die, but you could bring me back to life by not eating the Cave's food, and by going within in solitude, seeking to enhance your relationship with yourself above the Out'hers.

The only way you will revive me is to learn to survive by internal nourishment alone. You will need to do this for as long as it takes. This lesson that you live in the cave, you will teach the Out'hers, which will set them free from their enslavement by the Cave Guardian. So that is what the Cave Guardian meant when he said only YOU are welcome here.

SheyA knew she had to do this. She had learned to trust her heart.

So she gave up every material thing she had, as well as all of her senses, and stepped inside the cave. Upon entering, she felt her heart light dim and then slowly disappear.

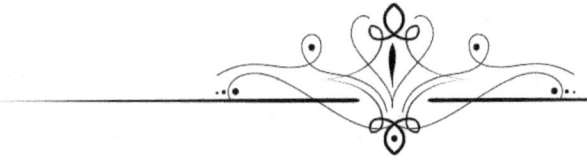

6 RE-AWAKENING

SheyA walked deeply into the cave, and before her, at the center of the cave, she saw a long table that seemed to go on forever. On it was a feast fit for a queen. She noticed all her favorite foods and quickly sat down to eat. But she did not seem to know how. Without a mouth, how would she eat? Then, one by one, the Out'hers came and greeted her by touching her body with a soft touch that made her skin crawl. Their masks looked so real in the cave that she forgot they wore masks in her world.

The Out'hers began to eat by putting the food directly into a small hole that led to their stomach. SheyA followed their lead and quickly got the hang of it. And they all ate and ate and ate. No one seemed to notice the Cave Guardian stayed outside the cave and was never in their midst.

They all ate until they were full. No one could not eat anymore. But no one was satisfied. The Out'hers went into the shadows, and SheyA fell asleep. The next day she woke up and felt hungrier than the day before.

Each day, a new feast would appear, and new Out'hers would join the table. Days passed, and SheyA remained in the cave, preoccupied with consuming, never satisfied, and hungrier the next day than the day before. There seemed to be something new every day, and she began to wait in anticipation for the next feast. There were some days she stayed up all night and never slept.

SheyA also felt a sense of grandeur that seemed to satisfy her need for belonging. She always had a place at the head of the table, and she began to crave the Out'hers' touch and the way they seemed to worship her. So much so, she forgot how dark the cave was, and that none of it was real. Time passed. No one knows how long. Some Shados say a year, but we know that to be an illusion.

Slowly a new desire began to awaken inside of her, and she began to feel that everyone in the cave was trapped. Slowly her special hearing began to whisper to her, and she began to hear the heart desires of the Out'hers. Some were deeply troubled and sad. Some were confused and angry. Some wished to go home to their real world.

SheyA knew that, deep inside, everyone in the cave wanted to go home, to their real homes. But none had the courage or the strength to fight through the pain of hunger and aloneness to be set free from the cave. For days, SheyA was tormented by their inner voices until she could not bear it any longer.

"I will stop eating, and nurture you back to life. Together we will get out of the cave, and I will go home," SheyA whispered into her heart. But how would she nurture her heart back? It could not survive because no one was real. Suddenly SheyA knew the answer. She had to look beyond the mask and see the real faces of these Out'hers. Seeing their actual faces was the only way her heart would see their true selves and come back to life.

So she gathered her courage, and finally one day, SheyA made up her mind to find a corner of the cave to go inwards and seek solitude. She would not eat a bite, regardless of what it was. She would connect with her heart daily for as long as it took so that she could look at the real faces of the Out'hers and not be tricked into believing their false selves.

7 HEART RESURRECTION

So SheyA began her solitude and fasting in the cave. At first, the Out'hers taunted and made fun of her. Their masks stayed on initially, but after a while, they began to deteriorate. SheyA now could see the Out'hers as they were. But she ignored them because she knew what they were feeling. Days passed into weeks as they tormented her with lies and fake gestures. Weeks passed into months, and finally, one day it all just stopped. Just like that. It stopped. No more noise or funny faces from the Out'hers. No more banquets. SheyA was alone in the cave. All had disappeared, and she was at peace.

She talked to her heart often, and it slowly began to respond. It was quiet for a long time. Then one morning, thump! Her heart had re-awakened.

SheyA's heart spoke to her softly, "Follow me and I will lead you out of the cave." SheyA began to walk as her heart guided her out of the cave. Shados say for 130 days SheyA lived alone in this cave, saying nothing and seeing no one. But we know that's an exaggeration.

Once SheyA made it out, the Cave Guardian was nowhere to be seen. She was tired, hungry, cold, and once again poor. SheyA asked her heart what to do. She could not image looking for her stuff in this huge pyramid of stuff. She would do without and leave it all. She had survived in the cave without stuff; she would survive out here as well.

Naked, tired, cold, and hungry, she continued her quest, turning inward often to listen to her heart. She eventually reached the base of a mountain and asked her heart, "Which way do we go?" Her heart responded, "Go RIGHT again, then up the side of the mountain. Walk as far as you can until you can walk no more." So she did.

8 SUN OF GOD

SheyA walked and walked. She walked so much she forgot
she was naked, tired, cold, and hungry. She noticed the more
she walked and climbed, the more she was becoming anxious
and angry. What a total waste of time, she thought. This
quest has been a waste of time. I'm no closer to finding what
I wanted, and I'm tired, hungry, thirsty... how can I go home
now? I'm naked, I've lost everything, and I have a bad
attitude. It was during this tirade of despair that she came
upon the Sun of God. It was shining so brightly; she could not
look directly into it. Her Spirit lifted, and she felt, lighter.
The only way she knew he was still there was that this Sun of
God was different. In her world, he did not cast a shadow,
but in the Out'hers' world, he cast a shadow on the land. So
that is where she looked to speak to him.

However, the Sun of God did not speak; his shadow pointed
to a building not so far from her. The building was not very
big, but it had two tall columns on each side with the words
"Library of Truths" etched in the stone façade. Somehow
SheyA knew that to enter, you must let go of your fears.

Somehow SheyA understood that she needed to go into this library of truths where she would find Wisdom, and then she could return home. She may not have had anything left, but she would at least go home with Wisdom. So she walked toward the building, took a deep breath to release her fear, and walked into the first large wooden door, followed by another door, then another.

SheyA had to pass seven doors in total, each a different color. Once inside, she realized that this library was much bigger inside than it appeared from the outside, and it seemed to go on forever. Straight ahead of her stood another door with a large red and white sign that stated, "The only way out is to know the whole truth. To know the whole truth, you must read every book in this library. Signed by: The Librarian of the Truth."

Deciding this was total nonsense, SheyA quickly turned around to try to make her escape, but it was too late. The doors behind her had disappeared as "magickly" as the building, and Sun God had appeared. She was trapped, and the only way to get out was to find Wisdom.

She knew she was never going to be able to read all these books. Hence, she was never going home, she thought. She was trapped in a library in search of Wisdom. How ironic. Someone needs to tell this story, she thought. Then she remembered her heart and how it had not failed her so far. So SheyA asked it once again, "What do I do?" Her heart said,

"Fill your mind with the knowledge contained in these books. Check with me every minute along the way without fail. Never turn a page without checking with me first to see how you feel about what is written. The Wisdom in these books will be revealed to you by the Shado in your darkest hour, and you will bypass the demand of the Librarian." So SheyA opened the most impressive book she could find and sat down to read.

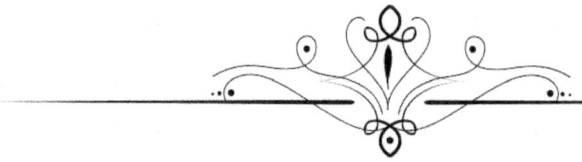

9 FINDING WISDOM AND GOING HOME

Without realizing it, SheyA has chosen the thickest, oldest book near her. Subconsciously, she thought this might be the smartest place to start. She digested every page and checked in with her heart often, though not as often as she used to do back home. As the hours passed, she practiced staying connected with her heart. With each book, she got better and better. She looked for every type of book she could find, and she read every page. She chose books by topic, color, and size. She made a game of it and would pick the most colorful, the thinnest, the fattest and everything in between. All the while, SheyA checked in with her heart to find if there was any truth in the pages. She periodically checked in to know how she felt along the way.

Days passed into weeks, and weeks into months, according to the Shado. But we know that is a stretch of the imagination.

SheyA read each book of truth, and when she would check in with her heart, her heart determined they all felt good, and there was truth in every one.

Freya fretted. How could this be? Every one of these books cannot be true! How will I find Wisdom if everything is true? This library is not going to help me find the Wisdom I seek.

SheyA began to doubt her heart, but fought the urge and kept forging ahead. She kept on reading and barely noticed with each book she opened; a new shadow would either appear somewhere in the library or come out of every book. Finally, she looked up, and there were shadows everywhere, one from every book she had read.

But, since she had left her fear as payment for Wisdom, SheyA was not afraid of the shadows. She began to remember that back in HeartLand; there was one Truth that everyone knew it. Everything that existed was a part of everyone, including these books. This is why no one ever needed or wanted for anything. All was always provided. As long as HeartLanders connected to their hearts, they were a part of part of everything, and everything was a part of them.

So, she put down her final book, number 401. She thought about what her heart had said before she entered the library. "The Wisdom in these books will be revealed to you by your Shado in your darkest hour." Now she understood her heart had whispered Shadow, not Shado. So she turned inside herself and asked her shadow, "Where is my Wisdom here?"

Her shadow answered, "We are everywhere and in every book. Like HeartLand, here we are also a part of everything and everything is a part of us. But here, we are disconnected and separated from our hearts. So to find light, you must search and acknowledge the shadow. "

"These shadows in this library of truth symbolize the un-truths and the void in these books. "

"These books are all true because the truth exists in everyone's heart and because the Out'hers are not connected to their hearts or anyone else's heart. The shadows too are disconnected and live as if separate from their source."

"Truth seekers here will never find the truth, but also the untruth."

SheyA's excitement quickly turned back into sadness. "But does this mean there is no truth and no lies? This means there is no wisdom to be found to take back home?"

SheyA thought, I found the Library of Truths only to discover that it's also the Library of Un-Truths. Everything here is disconnected and not whole. The Wisdom I found is that there's no wisdom at all.

It was at this point her heart whispered, "Look up and ahead of you now." Reluctantly SheyA looked up and ahead.

She saw the Moon Goddess light peeking through the window of the library. "SheyA, you are right. Here, nothing is real. Here, nothing exists. Follow me, and I'll show you how to walk through the door that goes unseen by man but seen by all new to this land. Then you can go home. Your home is the only place where Wisdom exists. Your home is the source of all there is."

SheyA asked, "What is the price that I have to pay? Everyone so far has wanted something. I have paid for everything I owned. Now I have nothing to show for my quest and nothing to pay you."

The Moon Goddess said, "Then NO thing is your price. I will take your nothing as your price. So SheyA, give me your nothingness, and you will be free to return home." And SheyA understood.

So SheyA gave the Moon Goddess her nothingness and waited. Not wanting to appear ungrateful after such a kind offer, SheyA waited. And waited. After a few minutes had passed, SheyA inquired, "But where is the door?

The Moon Goddess laughed.

"Woman, you are the door. Your womb is the door of man. To leave this place, you must return through the portal that birthed you into this land. Walk through your womb and up the stairway to your heart, and there, you will be home. "SheyA didn't understand. "But how? How do I walk into my body?"

"SheyA, my daughter," began the Moon Goddess. "You gave me your nothingness and no longer have a body. You have no things. You are only light. You can now go wherever you want, whenever you want. You just have to imagine your womb as a portal back to your heart and give birth to yourself in HeartLand."

So SheyA's heart, imagination, and fifth sense, all working together, imagined herself walking through her womb up to the spiral stairway, and back home into HeartLand.

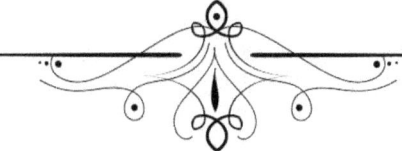

AUTHOR

Irmina Ulysse

Author Irmina Ulysse is a national speaker, ordained minister of metaphysics, a priestess and founder of Sodotutu™. Her work and books inspire us to embrace our inner nature to achieve balance and harmony.

For inquiries, visit www.sodotutu.net

www.ingramcontent.com/pod-product-compliance
Lightning Source LLC
Chambersburg PA
CBHW070652130626
46555CB00006B/2842